# A MORAL LESSON

D1440883

# Acknowledgements

This collection includes the complete text of *A Moral Lesson I*. My sincere thanks to Steven Ungar, Kaiama Glover, Max Winter, Omar Berrada, Sarah Juliette Sasson, Olivier Brossard, Cathy Leung, Yan Brailowsky, José Ramos, Jean-Philippe Mul, Christopher M. Jones, Sébastien Biot, Marie-Aude Preau, and Wyatt Mason for help, encouragement, and thoughtful readings of sections of the work at various stages of its development.

In the process of completing this project, I sometimes strayed from the suggestions of the above-mentioned individuals, who made their recommendations with care and generosity. I accept full responsibility for any instances in which the following translation falls short of its mark.

My gratitude also to the editors of *The Village Voice Literary Supplement, Jubilat, Double Change, Circumference, Poets & Poems* (a publication of the Poetry Project), and to Belladonna Books in collaboration with Boog Literature for first publishing some of these translations, occasionally in earlier versions.

—LISA LUBASCH

# Paul Éluard

# A MORAL LESSON

Translated from the French
by Lisa Lubasch

GREEN INTEGER
KØBENHAVN & LOS ANGELES
2007

GREEN INTEGER BOOKS
Edited by Per Bregne
København/ Los Angeles

Distributed in the United States by Consortium Book
Sales and Distribution, 1045 Westgate Drive, Suite 90
Saint Paul, Minnesota 55114-1065
Distributed in England and throughout Europe by
Turnaround Publisher Services
Unit 3, Olympia Trading Estate
Coburg Road, Wood Green, London N22 6TZ
44 (0)20 88293009

(323) 857-1115 / http://www.greeninteger.com
http://www.greeninteger.com

First Green Integer Edition 2007
English language translation ©2007 by Lisa Lubasch.
Originally published as *Une leçon de morale*
(Paris: Éditions Gallimard, 1949)
Copyright ©1949 by Éditions Gallimard.
Reprinted by permission of Éditions Gallimard.
Back cover copy ©2007 by Green Integer.
This work, published as part of a program of aid for publication, received support
from the French Ministry of Foreign Affairs and the Cultural Services of the French
Embassy of the United States. Cet ouvrage, publié dans le cadre d'un programme
d'aide à la publication, bénéficie du soutien du Ministère des Affaires Etrangères
et du Service Culturel de l'Ambassade de France aux Etats-Unis.

Design: Per Bregne
Typography: Kim Silva
Cover photograph: Paul Éluard

LIBRARY OF CONGRESS CATALOGING IN PUBLICATION DATA
Paul Éluard [1895-1952]
*A Moral Lesson*
ISBN: 978-1-931243-95-7
p. cm – Green Integer 144
I. Title II. Series. III. Translator

Green Integer books are published for Douglas Messerli
Printed in the United States on acid-free paper

# Table of Contents

# Preface

How many times have I changed the order of these poems, making "good" what was "evil" and vice versa? Did day follow night or night follow day? My moods are unpredictable, but dawn and dusk never falter. They transform themselves: the day bursts forth, and the night smolders behind its faded eye. The day speaks a clear language, in which one sees oneself. The night promises nothing.

My virtues, my failings, my optimism and my incompetence become entangled; I am only human. For me, the trick was not to think myself too virtuous, giving all to goodness *(or perhaps:* the trick was not to give myself over to sadness and not to destroy everything, and ultimately myself).

I wanted to be a moralist. How many times did I have to repeat to myself, with a soldier's absurd determination: "Evil makes you suffer or makes others suffer, but goodness is just and harmonious and wise, in every way, you know this, don't deceive yourself." Because it's always easier to adjust your standards for goodness than to name something evil. You can cheat in life, but you can't fool death.

### OF ACCEPTANCE SPEECHES

I hesitated, though the good is absolute, its voice clear. I am still far too committed to a career in misfortune. I don't have the gift of ease that paves the way for eloquent idiots, buffering them like so many pearls in so many oysters.

What speech? Not to mention, what award?

### SORROW

Shameful or not, my sensibility is already dated. Whether you perceive it or not, my blood often turns cold. I've overspent my vitality; each day I live now is one more day of youth than I expected. At the crossroads, at the turning point, I saw a dead body, her corpse, my death. I learned to live by it, to make it my first principle. No more frivolity.

A proverbial voice henceforth dictates to me:

after sorrow, happiness remains a basic premise, pessimism a vice. It adds nonchalantly: all truths are necessary to make a world.

## OF AN ETHICAL AESTHETICS

Can the clay jar be more beautiful than the water it holds, the beloved more beautiful than the lover, the vein more beautiful than the blood? Do you ever envision the earth separated from the sky? Can you imagine a hand without fingers, a soul without a body, a dawn without light, a conscience without a purpose?

Death eludes moral distinctions, for death alone has no form. I cannot escape it.

The claim that a graceful death brings eternal life is the ultimate abuse of language.

## OF REQUIRED OPTIMISM

Even in a ghost-like state, we keep performing. Force of habit, once established, keeps the dead going. We create duties for ourselves that persist after we die. Sometimes they last for a long time, we say proudly.

An underlying goodness sustains us, according to

the rhythms of life. For we have always wanted goodness. We anticipated the progression of our actions, adding a rung to the solid ladder of progress, sawing off a bar from our fragile prison.

## OF NATURAL OPTIMISM

At the outset, I thought like a champion. I was a new man. I saw before me a cloudless future.

And if the days I enjoyed were marred by innumerable nights, if I never knew triumph, I held on to the idea of it. In spite of everything, amid sorrow, danger, terror, I was able to see through to the other side of hope. Whether laughable, defenseless, exhausted, or idle, I relied on tomorrow. Otherwise, I could not have been born.

Like the last of the rapscallions, I imagined the impossible, the continuous life, happiness. And happiness answered me, from the depths of time. Its murmur became thunder, and rain poured from the wound. I conquered the fecund earth.

I live to improve myself.

No stage of life resembles death. Because we are not acquainted with our death. We always count ourselves among the living, and never among the dead, whom we do not count at all. In every street lined with ruins, a palace will rise. Where a skull was once streaked with wrinkles, a virgin brow now blushes. A trembling sea makes a sudden and steep rise, attacking the insoluble fog. Curving towards the earth, the harvest renews itself.

Space is measured in human terms. And time remains securely held in one arduous, everlasting spring.

*

Evil must be transformed into goodness. And by all the means we have left, so as not to lose everything. Through our perseverance, we will render pain and error harmless. Because we've always had faith.

I've wanted to deny, to destroy, the black suns of disease and misery, the bitter nights, all the pits of darkness and indeterminacy, the poor vision, the blindness, the destruction, the dried blood, the tombs.

I would have fought this fight even if I'd had only one moment of hope. Even if losing were certain. For others will win in days to come.

All others.

# A MORAL LESSON

*to Jacqueline
who brought me back to life*

# Everything Is One

*On the side of evil:*

Evening and the pincers of solitude
Evening in which everything has been said
Nothing offers a way out
Under the cold under the paleness
Of the weather like a cadaver
Here I play the tragic role of one resigned
The chess game of those who only pretend to live
A block of oblivion has filled up my empty hands
I no longer know how to have a body
I no longer know how to have a perfect face
I forget life I am atrociously exposed
I am stripped bare like an outline like a sketch
Under the raw night of a death sentence obstructed
Under the iridescence of derisory tears
No not submissive but exhausted
I am a man without seasons a man absent
Reduced to nothing a draft of a man left to the cemetery

And I deplore the pain because it was faithful
Changing and beautiful it split my forehead in two
Freezing always burning the same mortal heart
Everything already there in advance both love and death
In this old-fashioned world I've supposedly lived
A golden heart had to struggle and bleed to live
Autumn had a reason.


*On the side of good:*

Evening and the pincers of solitude
I want to confess everything
I blush to be in autumn
When I think I am in May
Tonight


Under the coolness under the heat under the color
Of living time amphoral
Under the fluctuation
Of November and of May
I strike poses
I pretend to be concerned about my past
Ever the nostalgic one
See what a convincing player I am

I make people smile and laugh
At the cult of my own melancholy

Oh but I really know how to cry
Like a let down child like an invincible man
They are equal when shrouded in injustice
They whom fire makes innocent
Whom hope makes heavy with countless leaves

I like to say yes I know how to agree
With the sea with the forest with only my ten fingers
With my eyes with my ears
For that is my desire that is my pleasure
I came to the light with a light step
I was not born alone
My nakedness had its sisters
And like water given over to these evening passions
I give birth to swarms of insects
I am the cloud ablaze

Dawn awakens and I awaken
And the promise of being happy
Follows my oath to be immortal
I follow myself and the human face
Has so many different aspects under the sun

I could be filled by them
The sap rises and the earth grows
And I win the most difficult battle
Everything is one the sea and the earth
And the light and the visible men
The future right now and without limits

All forms of life
Have molded my behavior
I come undone I untie myself
My dreams belong to the world
Luminous and perpetual
And I am obedient in the eyes
Of each child and of its mother
The young wheat of my love
Gives wisdom to all men
There is no heart that wishes to suffer
No heart that is not good not strong
Like the stalk that is ripe and fertile
Reveals our own light to us

The seeds follow the furrow
Of my love far off in time

In the past nothing but shadows
In the future no enemies

Nothing but hope and trust
The same good the same strength.

# Nusch

*On the side of evil:*

Nusch I miss you it is sudden
As if the tree could miss the forest

I have never written a poem without you
I am in a cold bath
Of solitude and misery
Words have the weight of rags on wounds
The images sparing and stubborn
All of what I say reflects an absence
I receive the present like a treasure the pickaxe
My pleasure now is to kill time

Masking itself with smoke the young wood burned
The leaves and flames were not visible
O you my great black star you become distant
Your circle is only a point in my vicinity

You my vision changed into an insensitive and
    blind thing

Do away with reflections echoes of deceit
Do away with my remorse for life
Take back the kisses I receive in vain.


*On the side of good:*

My love we were sleeping together
And we laughed in the morning
Together all the time we needed to live

An entire eternity
And the more I saw you living by my side
The more I mistook you for the dawn and the summer

Sleeping deeply dreaming higher
Awakening one for the other
Such is the law of innocence

And to live higher than our dreams
To be identical through trust
That was our pleasure

In a world always an instant too young

Could we foresee winter or our death
Considering ourselves fossils before the end of the
    long spring

Reason we were both embodying you gentle
Like a cheek under the blush of the first fire
Reason we were free we triumphed.

# The Hour Embraces Silence

*On the side of evil:*

Sound again bells of poison
The reasons
For the most hideous of punishments

They are engraved into the marble
Of the mother of tombs

Etched in the stone palms
Of the death that scrapes away at me

I love the mother of graves
With a love so intense it is destined for evil
An ancient love foul to the taste

*

You get to your bed through a quiet street
Lined with houses gray like all the houses

A quiet rusted street
That has never been young

And there the poet Despair
Despair with self-respect
Has a face like an egg

Seeing himself in the stream
His noble heart rises

The poet has no more seed
To cheat time

He no longer has a tongue
To lick his melancholy
Images remain secret

*

My fake delicate pearl
If you could only beg for your bread

To be human you need a voice
No one considers you rich or poor
You have neither fever nor health

24

You are no better than nothing but what can you
    do about it you are
Your empty solitude the urn of your body

You are in the eyes of others an extra
Facade glove monument mask

Still if it were life's revenge
Of course evil does not stem from you or from others

And in the sad sweetness of your closed past
The most deadly love is only as strong as its suffering

                              *


Mother death is authentic and genuine
Its rays make the dead forever dead
They circle around my love destined for evil
No oar underground and no river to cross
To comprehend space and mark presence

To live is nothing but to go from a body to
    its nothingness
From form to night and from sense to oblivion

To live is to miss everything and to miss oneself
Since I'm dying each and every time in what I love

I have never killed myself but I am being killed
I leave illusion to cowards to the uninitiated

Such pain makes insanity bearable
The blind man has seen his flesh shrink back

Ruins you are whole
In my field of vision
Like a pleasure stripped to its essence
Like pain that has ceased.


*On the side of good:*

From its gagged mouth
The hour embraces silence

A bee rolls on the ground
With its thousand sisters

And a thousand bees rise up
Towards the flower that summons them

*

Painful languishing
The sparrows of evening

Sustain a family
That knows only warmth

A single season sounds
The only worry happiness has

*

The moon multiplies
In a tree covered with mistletoe

The mistletoe that multiplies
The belly that reproduces

The tree becomes invigorated by it
Life is infinite

*

The man tears out the gag
And his heart fights the hours

His head mixes them up.

# Clock of Secret Weddings

*On the side of evil:*

Why must I always fall asleep
Why must the night devour me

I am unable to go without a halo
It hurts to be without a crown

But when I sleep soft chimes sound
My indolence hangs on their rope

I dream of the heart of my dead youth.

*

Then time gives birth to a new order
Order of fall with twisted foliage

I am born I die I open and close the door
I am at the heart of what dies from blooming

I do not know how to leave from where I start off
Nor how to see any part of my sad future

I decorate my sheets with my twisted scowl.


*On the side of good:*

Over the delicate sky enormous clouds
Broke the flow of monotonous dreams

And when the flaming storm made a face
I was breathing darkness I was taking form

I conceived the earth that I worship
I was like everything that I name

I fortified the forgiving earth.

*

A thousand songs of grapes and apples
Bedecked all words with fruit

A thousand voyages of animals and men
Sought out the day on the earth without limits

Night kissed the lips of dawn
The flowers were opening under the frantic light

I was radiance I was weakness and strength.

# O Endless Death

*On the side of evil:*

A scrap of joy is life's highest reward
All that's necessary is acceptance
With a sad smile as if after tears
You come away from it covered with a light dust

I have my skin my sheets my sorrow and my awakening
My ties and my work my doubts and my shame
I declare dead details become the whole
Forever I contain within me the time that passes
    through everything

And I have the thick earth where the root pushes
Where the day sinks in an avalanche towards my heart
I see from below where the owl recognizes its shadow
In the darkness of my night that divides the world.

*On the side of good:*

To be united is the farthest goal of the world
The heart of man expands
The end of the world comes nearer

The people's heart beats harder
The people's heart strikes the earth
And the harvest will be perfect

Our work is a challenge
Thrown out to the masters to the borders
We want to work for ourselves

We shall seize day in spite of night
We shall forget our enemies
Victory is dazzling

We have understood the secret of fire
It must give us health
We rise like stalks

And we plant the seed of love.

# Shadows

*On the side of evil:*

There were two of us heating ourselves at the same fire
Fire that burned the blood of tropical forests
And that made dry leaves rise up to the sky
Heavy flames from the den below the earth
They dance in the eyes behind the stars

There were two of us heating ourselves at the same fire
Weighed down with love as with lead as with feathers
In pain and in joy we were as one
Same color same smell same taste
Same passions same rest same balance

Our movements our voice unwound as one
The gold of our memory came from the same dross
And our kisses followed a similar path
I kissed you you kissed me I kissed myself
You kissed yourself without knowing exactly who
   we were

You were trembling all over in my trembling hands
We went down the same slope towards fire
Presence and absence towards fire
Towards its delirium and towards its ashes towards
    the end
Of our union the end of man with woman

How could we have ever felt separated
We who were weaving our days and our
    nights dreaming
Lovers of a common time lovers of twin flesh
Nothing changed meaning or accent for us
When we lay between the sheets we were useful

And on street corners we did not live in vain
We were fighting without doubts for a life
    of brotherhood
We were one with the wind with the sail
With the unlimited hope of unhappy men
They are at the end of everything and praise their birth

But you are dead and I am very much alone
I am cut off I ache I am cold I live
Despite the nothingness I live in denial

And if it weren't for you who lived
As a perfect being as I should be

I wouldn't even have to respect our shadows.


*On the side of good:*

Shadows on earth turning shadows
Obedient daughters of the sun
Dancers young and peaceful
Friends of man and beast

Shadows on earth shadows of night
Always darkest near the dawn
Like the others and the moon
Is very light to the pale sleepers

Shadows underground shadow of the miner
But his heart beats harder than his shadow
His heart is the thief of fire
He gives birth to our future.

*

Offense under the shadows
A shadow develops
Of disgust of misery
Of shame and of wrath

Working without hope
Digging one's own grave
Instead of lighting up
The eyes of one's fellow men

The miners said no
To defeat to ashes
They want very much to give
But who receives

The heart has no limits
But patience does
No one should know hunger
So that others can stuff themselves

Others who are apostles
Of the swallowed earth.

\*

Comrades in the mines I tell you now
My song has no meaning if your life is
   without purpose

If man must die before his time
The poets must die first.

## The Will to See Clearly

*On the side of evil:*

My discourse is obscure because I am alone
It is daytime
Very much so
Maybe it will be forever

Yet the door closes
On a dream of clarity
On the sun on the grass
On a face happy to be understood
To be accepted

Yet the door closes
On the happiness I wished for that I created
And I speak of night in spite of the noisy day
I forget the day of my dreams I cover myself in dirt

My name is nothing
And you took my name in tying yourself to me

Night I speak of death I believe in only the earth
Yes everything will exist the worst and the best

But I won't have been there.


*On the side of good:*

The totality of the day weighs down on the valley
Like an overabundance of fruit in a basket

Flame for flame day for day
Here one pictures oneself in light
And sky on earth
It is the will to see clearly

We do not lose a single blade of grass of hope
We refuse to be without dreams all winter long

For us the sun shines
We believe in spring it's never so far away
That we cannot reach it in the blink of an eye
The blind do not exist

Riverbanks of love for us are banks of justice
And the goal our hands seek

Our stream has its course
It is the heart the throat and the tongue and the voice
It goes forward always carrying meaning
Carrying our desire for an expansive tomorrow

Through the amorous body of instant happiness.

## Memories and the Present

*On the side of evil:*

I dreamt and I confess I dream much too much
For my own good because my dreams are dead ends

You were naked and beautiful and I felt compassion
You kissed me I had pity on my nocturnal self

I thought that nothing could light the way for me.

*

And time is responsible for everything
This time behind before during after past
My heart as it sleeps knows nothing of duration.

*

My justice on earth but even so you had only
A very light springtime to offer me to survive

As though we were two puffs of green
Setting free every bird from their sky-blue lips

We were never able to foresee anything except the sun.

*

There is no end to destruction
There is no end to my lamentation
You are dead this word has destroyed everything for me

Let negativity reign nothingness grows
Dark winter and the ancient snow of the grave.

*On the side of good:*

What I love embodies my desire to live
I took her in the present she stays in the present
Her soft nakedness scatters the light

Pure air passes more purely from her mouth to her eyes
She sees everything for me and I choose for her
The leaf at the heart of the tree and the clear spring

She is the tree and the leaf and makes the water overflow
We are born one for the other together at each dawn
And our laughter rubs out the desert of the sky.

*

We both know well that evil threatens us
But we are confident in the powers of love
She is my intention of living without regret
Of living without suffering of living without dying

I am luminous for she is filled with light
I love her through everything I know all the paths
For finding her again my lamb and my fleece
My sister and my strength my bond of blood

There is only one life therefore she is perfect.

*

Tenderness of the storm when it melts into the rain
And may the grain take hold beneath the sun and in
    the ground
The long night fades death greets life
The rainbow lives on blood under our skin

We are witnesses there have always been
Simple witnesses like us to testify for the good
We vow with our hands outstretched
That everything is ended that everything will begin

Without anything resembling what has been.

# The Seven Veils

*On the side of evil:*

In the flow of stone
In the resolute past

My life lasts for ages

In the flow of flesh
In the mother-of-pearl lung of water

In the vine of blood

In limbs planted
Deeper than my eyes

In the revered word

My life materializes
But also my reason for dying shamelessly.

*On the side of good:*

Gray dawn eyes made dull
Hunger quieted by alms

Wound bandaged by the enemy
Wound licked by a friend

The house inhabited even by disaster
Even torn-up roads

Soft hands damaged
Pink lips faded

A hunt without prey
A rope without a hanged man
A woman without children

The walls of my blindness
Everything surrounding my vision
A voice without question
A deafness in solitude

A hypothetical past
A certain future
A love that will end

    I regret nothing
    I move forward.

# In the Worst Conditions

*On the side of evil:*

I search for a pretense for love
A confession larger than my heart
A smile to make honey melt
A kiss for the unfortunate

I look for a body nothing less than a body
Just as hyenas seek decaying flesh
A stone on which the law is inscribed
For a body exposed nothing less than naked

And I sink down into the night
Wanting the earth I have its shadow
And as for fuller feasts
There death will consume my face.

*On the side of good:*

Love I hear a crowd

Shouting love so loudly it loses its voice
Love that rises in a single scream
All people become one living being

Love I am beyond
Love I am no longer embraced
Love I stumbled over your shadow

Love I have begged you too much
Caressed you too much exposed you too much
Love you left nothing but ashes

There are no more depths
Or summits there is nothing left
At the bottom of time but an unknown

United with men by moral obligation.

# Childhood the Teacher

*On the side of evil:*

Ah said he from the lowest point of the horizon of
  his memory
I came to the world in order not to age
Youth was enough for me I was expecting nothing else
I was living on light and I didn't think about it

And yet the light steals away and I know it

I was easing the unfeeling caress of my bare hand
Amidst the flowering of innocent flesh
I had the esteem of youthful brows of feverish eyes
I was conquering I was conquered and I was crying
  because of it

Today I am aware of my illusions

On the threshold of love I did not think that cares existed
And on the long table of the happy life
I brought the seasons together in a single measure
The forms of pleasure were limiting my thoughts

The place of my youth is inaccessible to me

I was young the rain watered my gardens
The smoke of the sun intoxicated my sleep
I was young I played like the breath of laughter
I had for the present the passion of the innocent

I am no longer the same the shadows have beaten me

No I was not drawn to becoming a man
My movements of hope were involuntary
Today the future is no longer born inside my heart
Tomorrow will be the first day after my death.


*On the side of good:*

From the first day when goodness
Takes a step again finds earth again
To the days overflowing with victories
My will defines itself

From the day when I feel prideful
To the days when I laugh at myself

Everything is corrected is transformed
I take on the proportions of a man

There are kisses for everyone
And a "thank you" from every mouth
The child shows the man
How to portion his pleasures

When summer dies winter begins
Stuffing the dawn with promises
Strength and weakness are of the same sex
The froth of life is virginal

And time passes and the future
Fixes and prolongs my desires.

## Unmoving Dawn

*On the side of evil:*

The woman had her day her hour her moment
I was the instrument

I said what she had to say
Nothing more

The woman had color warmth and poverty
Hunger thirst sleep flesh at the side of life

There is no challenge for woman
She stretches out on a straw mattress

She perishes in the ashes of flowers
Clearing and barricade love and hate

Her childhood reborn in a mass of fruits
Without image oh above all without image and
    without heart

Like a mirror that is never friend to man.

54

*On the side of good:*

Impure man is veiled who looks at the woman
He no longer sees his own architecture in the air

He sings through one eye he is delirious through
     the other
Quick he loses his hands inside the tournament of flesh

Glowing but weakened his expression is vague
What he was thinking straight ahead breaks down
     and becomes listless

The wave of woman shaped its beaches
He unfurls everywhere he sets his birds free.

                              *

He who truly looks at woman leaves no tracks
His shadow is on the earth like a heart without a body

Soft and strong outside of death his heart soars.

# I Love Her She Loved Me

*On the side of evil:*

I hate her I hate myself I love her and she loves me
We are ever friends and enemies

And I believe she never saw the light
In the eyes that smiled upon her

She burrows without feeling into deepest night
The nest where she may fade endlessly.

*On the side of good:*

Our heart beats for all humanity
And when I spoke your language I was speaking mine
Our ambiguous universe
Has but one open portal

We were little kings
But we were everyone's equals

Little children believing
All we were told

Yet our truth gave off an earthly sound.

# No Joke

*On the side of evil:*

Like a pearl in which the moon creates itself
Cold to the point of hardening winter's outline
Cold to the point of confusing flame and ash
Indifferent and forgetful to the point of dying

I could see her though she was moving alive and naked
I spoke her language she did not know mine
That evening she was unaware of my sentimental thirst
But the least reason for living is enough

She was the one who revealed the ruins
And the oblivion of ruins and the oblivion of mourning
Living and naked she shaped my rebirth
I needed to know everything of her disaster

In order to find again selfishly at nightfall
Low dawn and the quivering flower of daylight
On the vast horizon of the four seasons of life
Where man multiplies his image in his sons.

*On the side of good:*

She was slow she gathered sun and snow
Majestically
She mingled her body with other bodies
As one conjures a lover

She was tender and sweet she gave her hands
As a bird its song
She opened herself on a kiss and went away
In search of fair weather

She was strong and had no time to waste
On worries on torments
She joined the nakedness of precious stones
With the laughter of children

Immensely real she reinvented
A harmonized earth a mother earth
And eyes to see that all is worth seeing
Without derision like a pebble at the bottom of a well

And like a dead tree that makes the mistletoe
    more joyous.

# The Despair Need to Love

*On the side of evil:*

The storm abates the rain falls off
And the sun makes a hollow sound
Blow little pigs cry crows
Children drool in cellars

The black cold settles down in little windows
He who cannot fully live lives a little
Knowledge gives alms to ignorance
Rust has golden roots

Beautiful flesh is a thorn
The lip freezes in a kiss
One slides in the mud of the heart
The dead live in palaces

Whoever you are grab a weapon
And avenge yourself of this disaster
The mirrors have multiplied
So that one evening you cease to see yourself in them.

*On the side of good:*

How wondrous it is to love again
In spite of the endless wall
Like a miner who ponders day
During the day his heart inspires his climb
You are not there your body exists
And the stars of your hands
Although concealed are always present

See the poet transforms himself
I dream I have always dreamed
Of dusk in negative
And the wonder could have been
Not to have been born to be absent
But you are worth having been
And being in spite of nothingness

I know your breasts I know your heart
Your eyes that open in my eyes
Even though I am an old blind man in my dreams
To love you sing loudly enough at night
To light up a world
Other than that of my own life
Loving you links me with mankind.

## Last Day of Winter
## First Day of Spring

*On the side of evil:*

We lie in the straw
We dreamt a long time ago
To stretch to infinity
On the lace of sense

We dreamt of seeing in the abyss of sense

There were the eyes of others
There was stupidity
Ignorance and clouds of understanding
The origin and the end
My heart and yours

Last day of winter
First day of spring
Two worlds belonging only to us
Two worlds that always haunted us

We wanted to confuse them

She is dead and life tell me what am I expecting from
    the world
Today I am ready to grasp my pain
We dreamt a long time ago today I want to live

I lost my reflection in the abyss of sense
My night disturbs the night but no longer waits for
    the day
I am at the point of death I have no future

We lie in the straw
Halfway unhappy without thinking about it
A knowingly unhappy man lies on a dung heap

It's nice out it's dark out
Darkness is the rule
We dreamt a long time ago
We were wrong to live one does not have to dream

One must settle for being tired out before it's time.

*On the side of good:*

The heavy breast of the sun
Offers itself to my lips through your lips
To my hands through your providing hands
From all your flesh to my body

My desire is greater than the sky and the sea

From being doubled and divided
We feel stronger we command the day
And the pleasures of the day and the pains of the day
Our heart covers all horizons

My desire my love fits between your pure eyes

And our scenic caresses
Our first kisses of spring
Our heavy embraces like storms
Unite the four elements

Behold the warmth behold my song that makes
    you eternal.

# Dreams

*On the side of evil (December 8, 1948):*

The domain of the caress is for the animals
I placed it in your hands
So that the animals would never be deprived of it

The domain of speech is for lovers
I settled down there I am alone there I am weary of
    life there
The dreamers wait at the door mouths open

They will never get possession of the truth
The truth a caress here and there and the bitterness
They will have only words deforming mirrors
From which they will never leave.

*On the side of good (April 27, 1949):*

O impossible wonder with no birth and no end
I have known the wonder of being paralyzed

And of being full of life absent complete present
Every desire was rubbing against me was turning
    itself on
Every desire was rising inside me was flowering
I was struck by lightning rain and sunlight
I was blind I was curving my rainbow
Over the mane of the harvest over the houses
    and windows
Over harsh peaks over extended hands
I was paralyzed I was blind and without a past
Without tomorrow I had a desire to know everything
At once and without moving an inch
I was lying down I was standing up dead and alive
As one thinks of oneself dead as one feels oneself alive

Love around me was shivering was exhausting itself
And was renewing itself like leaves in the woods
My five senses were mingling in a single flight
    their chains
I was the prey and the hunter who kneels down
The master who forgets his reasons for ruling
The diamond that shines beyond its stone casing
I was perfuming my eyes my tongue and my ears
With everything that passed along the banks of darkness
Day by day the exchanges were not always easy

But for me the one lying dead they were eternal
Young or old they were carrying my mark
There was great confusion in the world
But I was in order I was melding time
In full flesh I was uniting sperm and bones


To tell the truth my hands were trying to express
   themselves
They hurt me
To tell the truth I would have liked them to guide me
To tell the truth the woman was really that woman
And not another and my pleasure was born from hers
I used her belly to unify life
To tell the truth the woman had a female companion
As well as a male companion
A blind fervor was spreading with the wish to live
Without knowing where blood rushes out and
   becomes dry
To tell the truth the dead woman immortalized the
   living woman
To tell the truth lead sounded like gold
A woman switched off the nothingness beneath
   her shadow
And I the obscure one I had the answer to light.

# Bad Night Good Day

I dream I obey the orders of the night
I change the newborn feathers of my birth to lead
I make a pure crystal a deaf crystal in darkness

Silence grows along the dead branches
In dreams the whiteness of your flesh burns me.

                              *                    .

The sun enters the heart of the trembling room
Behold our love that doubles in the broad daylight that
    embraces itself
And its long caress makes us understand everything

The cool fire of dawn is filled up from a single body
Yours I am blinded enough to believe in it.

# Lazarus

I

The evening vanishes it is now night
Savage and dark opened on an absent world

The world of tomorrow must be reinvigorated
But without aging if I have aged nothing will be

From neither day nor night will sap ever run
If I do not have within me the strength of a young man

I have aged I no longer have the taste for anything
   but night
For the desert without fire without light without voice

Embittered poisoned the night slides into me
My mouth corrupts itself on kisses of nothingness

No part of me aches and I know it is wrong
My body is harrowed my destruction is certain

The night eats away at fruit the night is my assassin.

II

A signal the smoke in the sun
My heart thaws
A word a lone swarm of bees
My heart so dead returns to the world

Even vermin are magical
In my ten fingers
Winter peopled fertile and white
In my eyes enlarged by ecstasy

The nights learn how to walk
Dawn stutters
The rival life is armed again
I leave the cradle from the grave

Tears my tears warm me
My feet go forward
Already I feel the sun on my head
The good sun multiplies me

Already I store it
Against forgetfulness
For my daughters for my mothers
Already I feel immortal

Sun and moon
Are man and woman wed
I see sun I see darkness
I live I am free to see.

### III

For one tutor one hundred orphans
Everything is destroyed
And for one hero one hundred victims
I am defeated

I endure horrifying wounds
Blood stains me
I laugh as oafish as a coward
Mud erases me

Ardor fades I am mortal.

*

No importance the sky gives in
The earth wins
And on my evil shadowy bed
Hope survives every suspicion

The others will be granted life without suffering
And without burial
They will not pass through where I have passed
They will know nothing of the charms of death

Daylight on their hearts forever more
Daylight on their bodies
Daylight on the works of their hands
Nothing more will be destructible.

# On Animal Scale

A bull like a wheel
Far from sand far from water
And in his bright red eye
The club takes root

A bull aiming at the ground
Like a bow like a sword
Splits the man down the middle
Constructing in blood

The foundations of the sun.

## II

Fair weather is prey to wind
The grass is prey to good animals

Between the horns of the bull
Flows forth the spring of blood

The living source foaming
The fists clutching a treasure

And the light without a past
That never knows death.

### III

Between the open arms of the bull's horns
Weight and lightness balanced
The sun extends its mirror
To the black torches of fear

Glory a bull goes out in the grass
To thread a harmony of masses
And his flesh is a battle
Already won by the heart.

# The Language of Colors

I know you colors of men and women
Fresh flowers rotten fruits decomposed haloes
Prisms musicians mists sons of night
Colors and everything is vibrant opening my eyes widely
Colors and everything is gray that gives me something
    to cry about

Colors of health of desire of fear
And the sweetness of love gives an answer to the future
Colors crime madness rebellion and courage
Laughter everywhere exposing happiness
Sometimes reason that spits us out as imbeciles

Always reason that recreates us as sublime beings
The pulse of blood through the paths of the world
Colors and despair may very well dig vainly into
    the night
Mysteries darken insomnia stripping it down
But dreams will always seem beautiful and virtuous

On one side of my heart misery subsists
On the other I see clearly I hope and I become iridescent
Fertile I reflect a body that extends itself
I struggle I am drunk with struggling to live
I ground my victory in the brilliance of others.

# The Great Voyage

The great voyage of growth that I have made
In spite of so many evil spirits

Nature always goes forth towards its birth
And I have been absorbed into the image of dawn
And legions of birds were opening their
    resounding hearts
By shaking off their feathers and their song on the grass

The morning waves were rising one by one
The flowers shared the colors of noon
I was very happy I felt fresh and prepared
I was advancing fully shining everywhere

On the rising dew and on the fruits of the sun
I was right I was living well

Because I had made a great voyage of passion
Although everything worked against me

From the daybreak from your shoulder to your
    keyhole eyes
From the groove of your mouth to the harvest of
    your hands
From the region of your brow to the climate of
    your breast
I reanimated the shape of my sentient body

And thanks to your smiles that washed away my blood
I again saw clearly in the mirror of day
And thanks to your kisses that linked me to the world
I found myself again weak like a child

Strong like a man and worthy of leading my dreams
Towards the sweet fire of the future.

# The Beauty of the Devil

Everywhere beauty shines like a tree
The first tree of trees except in the cemetery
I am a tranquil victor

But if I accept the beauty that wanders joyless
In creatures childless unconsoled
I refuse myself desire

I want subtle or glorious naked beauty
The transmutation of evident grace
In a virginal breath of air

Beauty too often is an obscure lamp
I exalt it and give it the faint light of dawn
So that it may escape from the weakness of the moon.

\*

Little wings of birds traps of pearls
I immerse you in the crimson of the grapes of blood
The spring lures the green grass

Here and there eyes are poked out
And limbs lie frozen on layers of stone
And hair is caught on brambles

In the arteries wonders of dust
And leaden flames in the extinguished fires
Abuses under the eyelids

But the fierce beasts of summer are roaring
    and flourishing
Winter's sheets of ice are perfectly saintly
The nights and lights mingle in my head.

                    *


In the spring there are only beneficial gifts
And yet I see day and night from the perspective
    of survival
I want always to be happy

My senses are confused by my nascent past
I see myself always young nuptial welcoming
I am a witness to my childhood

80

Here are men born to be condemned
To death without hope and here children
Willing to survive on their dreams

Children marking the steps of their dance on earth
Dark and limpid their smiles lull them
Like a flame their youth caresses them.

## And He Who Spoke from Afar
## Was Given an Answer from Nearby

*The enemy:*

The day filters through ruins
Better than through gullible eyes
And the crops burn better
In the hands of the arsonist
Than in the grip of the sun

The mineworker digs his own grave
Work aggravates hunger
I am the master they bow down to me
Lower than the earth I crawl on
Where concealed I destroy

I count on death to live
O ruins love is a phantom
The world tolls nothingness
And on the bodies of my children
I annihilate time with a zero.

*The friend:*

The same tall blue wave
Carries the day for all men
Their future and their presence
And their charitable hope

Youth covers over old age
I need hands inside mine
Need a heart to feel myself alive
If I am alone the dawn is worthless

My sweet streams of spring
Tenderly open the earth
Fertile love laughs at the angels
At all the lovers of tomorrow

Revenge is a very small word
For these children who know they will live
Happiness is essential to them
It sings forever in their veins

They have won.

# Everything Is Saved

Everything is destroyed I can already see the disaster
A rat is on the roof a bird in the cellar
The mouths of books no longer murmur
All the paintings are turned upside down
Memories and witnesses blur themselves together

An old man is laying himself to rest a worthless doll near
    a cradle
A child bites down on the wreckage of a machine's gears
In the pit of a cemetery a cadaver has remained intact

And the sweet words of lovers and the lullabies
And the works make a shattering silence
The swallows in sight have closed their wings
A little purple fire has ripped apart Marie
An excremental breath rubbed out Max and Pierre

The defunct hell is drying on the steeple spires
A halo of shade strangles all brows
A hero bathes in the blood of a criminal

The hour comes to a standstill over the sewer and over
   the ocean
A blue leprosy eats away at the last trees
It is raining it is not raining and the clear day grimaces
Perhaps there has never been anything on earth
Since death flaunts itself like birth

Everything is destroyed I can already see the shambles
Where everything has ended the plow and the scythe
Have seized bundles of nerves with their beaks

The mirror of the comical mischievous genius
Reflects in its pool of lava a pathetic weapon
Has the dawn ever been compared to the very first desire
Have we ever learned how to read on the flank of a
   full belly
Was man made of stone and woman of ashes

A breast that once was glorious endures the caress
Of the cobblestones of a much traveled street
   disappeared
And the map of the city is covered with dust

Evil was searching out its partner for a strange
    engagement
And found him now the desert is here forever and ever
I picture him as he is shown to me black on white
Born in winter I am able to see the negative image
    of everything
I was born to die and everything dies with me

The extinguished stars seem to belong to me
Mourning unites the walls that keep men apart
No one to draw the moral from the story.

                        *


Nothing is destroyed all is saved we want it
We are in the future we are the promise
Here is tomorrow that reigns today on earth

There are hearty laughs in the open squares
Colorful laughs in gilded squares
Boats full of kisses explore the universe
The children the harvests vindicate ambition
Humankind gives strength to the conscience of mothers

Faces are moved by the brightness of passion
In their eyes freshness turns its feathered wheel
Carefree dreams wander all the roads

The desires are simple and the problems resolvable
The heart has so much space that it defies the stars
It is like an endless wave
It is like a spring that makes flesh eternal
The grandeur of life disavows death

I speak of the moment at which we've arrived
We want it and we won't give up for anything
We were going forward we have moved ahead

The miners have sung out against unjust punishment
The convicts have sung and shaken off their shackles
Our brothers have fought everywhere and without
    doubting themselves
And buds were emerging from the dry wood and
    the brambles
And bravery went hand in hand with love

Waking up oppressed intensified the struggle
We were less than nothing but we became everything

The world being ours we owned ourselves

The tongue of life melted in our mouths
We knew neither oasis nor shelter
We were seeking the uninterrupted brotherhood of
    the real
The concrete truth the tangible virtue
From the depths of pain we denounced evil

Our brothers were hungry were plundered
Driven to despair led to the slaughterhouse
But the rose of fire of their blood lived on

Men survived we were the proof
And the sons of their sons lit the future
Our accountants broke down the zeros of nothingness
Our farmers counted the months of genesis
Sight was extended into the distance like a radiant body

Our strengths here below had no limits
Beauty trust did not carry much weight
But today their dew is fertile

Here is tomorrow that reigns today on earth
On the day of forgiveness man is indispensable
And now the world becomes a useful thing
Voluptuous object indestructible and magisterial
Filled with life and with humanity.

2004

André Breton *Earthlight* (GI 102) [France]
Paul Celan *Breathturn* (GI 111) [Bukovina/France]
Paul Celan *Threadsuns* (GI 112) [Bukovina/France]
Paul Celan *Lightduress* (GI 113) [Bukovina/France]
Reina María Rodríguez *Violet Island and Other Poems* (GI 119) [Cuba]
Amelia Rosselli *War Variations* (GI 121) [Italy]

2005

Ko Un *Ten Thousand Lives* (GI 123) [Korea]
Vizar Zhiti *The Condemned Apple: Selected Poetry* (GI 134) [Albania]
Krzysztof Kamil Baczyński *White Magic and Other Poems*
(GI 138) [Poland]
Gilbert Sorrentino *New and Selected Poems 1948-1998* (GI 143) [USA]

2006

Maurice Gilliams *The Bottle at Sea: The Complete Poems* (GI 124) [Belgium]
Paul Éluard *A Moral Lesson* (GI 144) [France]
Attila József *A Transparent Lion: Selected Poems* (GI 149) [Hungary]
Nishiwaki Janzuburō *A Modern Fable* (GI 151) [Japan]
Takamuro Kōtarō *The Chieko Poems* (GI 160) [Japan]

GREEN INTEGER
Pataphysics and Pedantry

Douglas Messerli, *Publisher*

Essays, Manifestos, Statements, Speeches, Maxims,
Epistles, Diaristic Notes, Narratives, Natural Histories,
Poems, Plays, Performances, Ramblings, Revelations
and all such ephemera as may appear necessary
to bring society into a slight tremolo of confusion
and fright at least.

\*

Individuals may order Green Integer titles through PayPal
(www.Paypal.com). Please pay the price listed below plus $2.00
for postage to Green Integer through the PayPal system.
You can also visit our site at www.greeninteger.com
If you have questions please feel free to e-mail
the publisher at info@greeninteger.com
Bookstores and libraries should order through our distributors:
USA and Canada: Consortium Book Sales and Distribution
1045 Westgate Drive, Suite 90, Saint Paul, Minnesota 55114-1065
United Kingdom and Europe: Turnaround Publisher Services
Unit 3, Olympia Trading Estate, Coburg Road, Wood Green,
London N22 6TZ UK

\*

Cole Swensen *Noon* [1-931243-58-1] $10.95

Fiona Templeton *Delirium of Interpretations* [1-892295-55-5] $10.95

Henry David Thoreau *Civil Disobediance* [1-892295-93-8] $6.95

Rodrigo Toscano *The Disparities* [1-931243-25-5] $9.95

Mark Twain [Samuel Clemens] *What Is Man?* [1-892295-15-6] $10.95

César Vallejo *Aphorisms* [1-9312243-00-x] $9.95

Paul Verlaine *The Cursed Poets* [1-931243-15-8] $11.95

Mark Wallace *Temporary Worker Rides a Subway*
        [1-931243-60-3] $10.95

Barrett Watten *Frame (1971-1990)* [Sun & Moon Press:
        1-55713-239-9] $13.95
        *Progress / Under Erasure* [1-931243-68-9] $12.95

Mac Wellman *Crowtet 1: A Murder of Crows and The Hyacinth Macaw*
        [1-892295-52-0] $11.95
        *Crowtet 2: Second-Hand Smoke and The Lesser Magoo*
        [1-931243-71-9] $12.95
        *The Land Beyond the Forest: Dracula and Swoop*
        [Sun & Moon Press: 1-55713-228-3] $12.95

Oscar Wilde *The Critic As Artist* [1-55713-328-x] $9.95

William Carlos Williams *The Great American Novel*
        [1-931243-52-2] $10.95

Yang Lian *Yi* [1-892295-68-7] $14.95

Yi Ch'ŏngjun *Your Paradise* [1-931243-69-7] $13.95

Visar Zhiti *The Condemned Apple: Selected Poetry*
        [1-931243-72-7] $10.95

# The America Awards

FOR A LIFETIME CONTRIBUTION TO INTERNATIONAL WRITING
Awarded by the Contemporary Arts Educational Project, Inc.
in loving memory of Anna Fahrni

The 2006 Award winner is:

JULIEN GRACQ (LOUIS POIRIER)

[FRANCE] 1910

Previous winners:

1994 AIMÉ CESAIRE [Martinique] 1913
1995 HAROLD PINTER [England] 1930
1996 JOSÉ DONOSO [Chile] 1924-1996 (awarded prior to his death)
1997 FRIEDERIKE MAYRÖCKER [Austria] 1924
1998 RAFAEL ALBERTI [Spain] 1902-1998 (awarded prior to his death)
1999 JACQUES ROUBAUD [France] 1932
2000 EUDORA WELTY [USA] 1909-2001
2001 INGER CHRISTENSEN [Denmark] 1935
2002 PETER HANDKE [Austria] 1942
2003 ADONIS [Syria/Lebanon] 1930
2004 JOSÉ SARAMAGO [Portugal] 1922
2005 ANDREA ZANZOTTO [Italy] 1921

The rotating panel for The America Awards currently consists of Douglas Messerli [chairman], Will Alexander, Luigi Ballerini, Peter Constantine, Peter Glassgold, Deborah Meadows, Martin Nakell, John O'Brien, Marjorie Perloff, Joe Ross, Jerome Rothenberg, Paul Vangelisti, and Mac Wellman.

† Author winner of the Nobel Prize for Literature
± Author winner of the America Award for Literature
• Book translation winner of the PEN American Center Translation
   Award [PEN-West]
* Book translation winner of the PEN/Book-of-the-Month Club
   Translation Prize
+ Book translation winner of the PEN Award for Poetry in Translation